FIVE GO BUMP IN THE NIGHT

Other adventures in this series:

Enid Blyton

FIVE GO BUMP IN THE NIGHT

Text by
Bruno Vincent

Enid Blyton for Grown-Ups

Quercus

First published in Great Britain in 2017 by

Quercus Editions Ltd
Carmelite House
50 Victoria Embankment
London EC4Y 0DZ

An Hachette UK company

A CIP catalogue record for this book is available
from the British Library

ISBN 978 1 78648 477 2

This book is a work of fiction. Names, characters,
businesses, organizations, places and events are
either the product of the author's imagination
or used fictitiously. Any resemblance to
actual persons, living or dead, events or
locales is entirely coincidental.

Text by Bruno Vincent
Original illustrations by Eileen A. Soper
Cover illustration by Ruth Palmer

10 9 8 7 6 5 4 3 2 1

Typeset by CC Book Production

Printed and bound in Germany by GGP Media GmbH, Pößneck

FIVE GO
BUMP IN
THE NIGHT

CHAPTER ONE

A long, keening howl rose into the night sky.

There was a rustle as Julian sat up in his sleeping bag.

'What the bloody hell was *that*?'

'Oh, please, Julian,' said Anne, 'you're waking me up. It's just a woodland noise. Go back to sleep.'

'How can I sleep when hordes of ravening beasts surround us? First those murderous owls screaming their faces off, now this!'

'Ugh,' said Anne, sitting up. 'That's it. Now I'm awake.'

'Us too,' came voices from the other tent.

'It's for the best,' said Julian. 'Then, at least, when we get attacked, we'll have a chance to fend them off.'

'Don't be silly,' said Anne. 'It was probably just Timmy trying to make some friends out there.'

'You mean get his end away?'

Anne flicked on the torch and shone it in Julian's face.

'I did mean that, yes,' she said quietly, 'but I was choosing not to say it.'

'Woof,' said Timmy from nearby, his voice muffled.

'He's in there with you, is he?' asked Julian, unzipping the tent. 'Then I was right: there's a pack of slathering hell-beasts on the prowl.'

'Look, the fire's still going,' said Anne, peering out of the tent. 'I'll put some more wood on it. Maybe I could boil the kettle, make some peppermint tea or something.'

'Any of those ciders left?' Dick asked, joining them.

Julian shook the bag, which produced a reassuring clonk. He put one each in the outstretched hands of Dick and George.

'Too dark to read, and no telly,' said Julian.

'We could just have a nice old-fashioned conversation,' suggested Anne.

They all looked at the fire, which popped and spat.

'Tell a ghost story, then?' said George.

'Not with Julian as nervous as he is,' said Anne.

Another long, slow howl drifted up from the centre of the nearby woodland. Everyone shifted closer together on the log.

A long, keening howl rose up into the night sky.
'What the bloody hell was that?' yelled Julian.

'Why did we come camping, anyway?' Julian asked.

'Because Fanny and Quentin suggested it,' said Anne. 'They said they've got visitors and there's no room for us.'

'We could have just pitched a tent in the garden,' said Julian.

'That's true,' said George. 'But they did seem unusually keen to have us away from the house. I wonder what's going on . . .'

They all jolted as they heard some rustling in the foliage nearby. Timmy leapt up and stood alert, growling.

'Now we're all getting jumpy,' said Dick. 'Someone tell a story.'

'Yes,' said Julian, pulling his sleeping bag around his shoulders. 'Anything to take our minds off the fact we're about to get torn limb from limb. Even a scary story can't be worse than this.'

'All right,' said Anne. 'I've got one. Are you sure you can handle it, though?'

Dick blew a raspberry, and George told her to bloody get on with it.

'You too, Timmy?'

'Woof,' said Timmy.

'All right, then, I'll begin. It's about a group of young people very much like ourselves. In fact, I might as well make it simpler by giving all the characters our names. This is a story which I like to call . . .'

An American Werewolf in Dorset

It was a quiet, ordinary Tuesday evening (Anne began), and the four cousins – five, including Timmy – were down in Dorset, house-sitting for their aunt and uncle.

After dinner that evening, feeling the night was still young, they set off in search of a pub. They crossed fields and navigated paths, and even jumped a stream or two, until eventually they spotted in the distance what was unmistakably a public house.

'Hurray!' said Julian. 'First round's on me.'

'First round's on *me*,' said George, 'as long as you promise to drink a pint of water between beers. You finished off the best part of a bottle of plonk over dinner and I'm not bloody carrying you home.'

Julian opened his mouth to protest his sobriety – but hesitated. Now they were closer to the pub, he was arrested by the sign. It sported an impressively gory

illustration, beneath which was the legend: *THE BUTCH-
ERED CALF*.

'What a horrible name for a pub,' said Anne.

'I like it, it's excitingly gruesome,' said George.

Julian pushed the door open and found rather a cosy,
old-fashioned locals' watering hole, with a thick carpet,
brass fittings and a ceiling so low that even Anne had to
duck.

In the dim light, no one was visible except the barman,
who seemed to have been dozing until they arrived, where-
upon he came alive and started assiduously picking things
up and putting them down.

George ordered drinks and they sat down, looking
around at the chintzy wallpaper and curtains, and the
cheap watercolours and historical photographs in their
ornate gilt frames.

'Not much atmos,' whispered Dick.

'Hardly any customers,' said Anne. 'How does this place
stay open, do you think?'

'Maybe people are scared away by the legend of the
local werewolf,' said Julian.

The others turned tired glances towards him, but saw

'Oh, please, Julian,' said Anne, 'go back to sleep.'
'How can I sleep when hordes of ravening beasts surround us?'

he was looking at a newspaper cutting on the wall. He stood up to read it more closely.

'What's it say?' Dick asked.

'Reports of livestock mysteriously savaged,' said Julian in a tone of mild boredom. 'People missing – drawn, no doubt, to the bright lights of Bournemouth. Reports that it began after a secretive American research laboratory was established here during the Second World War. Ha! Load of rubbish.' He sat back down. 'Didn't you get any pork scratchings?' he asked George.

George shook her head. 'You get them,' she said. 'And I'll have some scampi fries.'

Anne made a face of someone about to be sick. 'They're both hideous.'

Julian got up, weaving slightly from side to side, and made his way to the bar. 'I'll have a packet of roast ox crisps. And . . . Have you got any Cheese Moments?' As the barman picked slowly through the basket of snacks, turning each packet over and holding it up to the light, Julian added, 'Hey, is this pub really named after the myth of the local American werewolf?'

The barman seemed to stiffen momentarily. Even in his

befuddled state, Julian could detect a sudden coolness in the room.

He looked around and saw that, when the five had entered, thanks to the very dim lighting, they had failed to see that there *were* a few drinkers huddled in the corner of the pub. They were elderly men, small and wizened, in farmers' tweed jackets and flat caps. And although Julian hadn't noticed them talking, their silence seemed loud by comparison, and he couldn't help but feel their eyes on him. Perhaps he'd been misheard, Julian thought. He laughed nervously.

Julian also noticed a newcomer, a youngish but impressively large man, at the far end of the bar. He had the wedge-shaped build of the American footballer, without needing any of the supplementary padding, and wore a jacket in the colours of the Milwaukee Maulers, or some such team (Julian couldn't make it out in the gloom). He was morosely nursing a drink – evidently not his first.

'What did you say about America?' asked the young man, aggressively.

'Nothing, nothing,' said Julian, handing over some coins for the crisps and tottering back to his table.

Anne, George and Dick did their best to defuse the tension in the pub by engaging Julian in brisk and lively conversation. This worked for a while – an hour and two more drinks, in fact – before, quite by accident, the conversation stumbled once more onto the topic of the werewolf.

'You don't think it's true, do you, George?' Anne asked, seeking reassurance from this bastion of staunch common sense.

George hesitated.

'Oh, you *can't*,' said Anne. 'It's so stupid. You might as well say Dracula exists, and . . . and—'

'Dracula did exist,' Julian pointed out. 'Vlad the Impaler. Whether he was a vampire or not, he was a real bloke.'

'So what?' said Dick. 'Michael J. Fox exists. Doesn't mean werewolves do.'

'Well, obviously I don't *believe* it,' said George. 'But, living out here in the sticks, you do get to hear some pretty weird and spooky stuff.'

'Like what?' said Anne.

George took a sip of her drink. 'When I was growing up, we had neighbours who regularly lost livestock, and even pets – and there were pretty grisly discoveries afterwards.'

'And, I've never admitted this before,' said Dick, 'but often, when I've been staying here and can't sleep at night, I've heard howling. You've heard it too, Anne, I know you have. It's horrible.'

Anne refused to acknowledge this. Her attempt to reassure everyone about this nonsense was backfiring badly. She pretended to be distracted by folding her scarf in her lap, over and over.

Talk quickly moved on, however, and soon enough from the slurring of his speech it became evident that Julian was not sticking to his 'one water, one beer' promise. And the attitude of the man at the bar was beginning to rankle with him.

Presently, he started on the topic of American politics, to the open horror and disdain of his fellow drinkers. What's more, he began to inveigh on the subject without taking care to do so quietly.

'HEY!' said a voice.

Now everyone at the table caught sight of the American visitor. He was a truly remarkable specimen, and practically oozed testosterone. Although only in his twenties, he had grown out his whiskers to a length that made Hugh Jackman appear positively girlish by comparison, and the sports jacket he wore bulged like a tarpaulin drawn tight over a bouncy castle.

'What was that?' he yelled. 'What were you saying about America?' Like Julian, he was far from sober, and seemed to have been drinking since lunchtime.

'I was simply observing . . .' Julian began.

'Time to go,' said Anne, placing herself between the man and Julian, and forcing her brother's coat on over his arms.

'Yes, is that the time?' asked George, getting up and shoving Dick out of his seat. 'Must be getting back.'

Julian allowed himself to be bundled to the door and out of it. As they walked the path across the field, away from the pub, the others felt with every step the intense stare from the man in the pub doorway.

'No!' said Julian. 'No, wait! I want to talk to that guy.'

'Julian,' said Dick, 'if you go back there, he's going to turn you into a hamburger.'

'Yes,' said Anne. 'He's obviously as thick as two short planks and out of his tree on booze. Let's leave it.'

'No,' said Julian. 'Seriously.'

'We're *being* serious,' said George. 'Let's just keep going. If you really want to get knocked out, there are some surgical spirits back at the house. Drink those. That's much safer than taking on Jocktimus Prime.'

But Julian was determined to go back.

The others first tried to reason with him, then they begged, then they threatened, and at last they lost their temper with him. He had been testing their patience for the past weeks and months, and, all of a sudden, they discovered where the limit of that patience was.

'Go, then!' Anne said. 'Go and get your head pummelled in. See if I care. You always ruin everything!'

'Why don't I knock him out now?' asked George, flexing her fist. 'It's for his own good, save him a worse beating . . .'

'Nah,' said Dick. 'There has to be a good chance that he won't actually get murdered. And it'll teach him a lesson. Besides, imagine trying to lump him all the way home.'

'Good point,' said George. 'I did warn him.'

14

The barman, who seemed to have been dozing until they arrived, came alive and started assiduously picking things up and putting them down.

So saying, they advanced into the velvety blue-black of the Dorset night, while behind them Julian tottered from foot to foot, blinking slowly, nodding, and sporadically remembering and forgetting again what it was he was determined to do next.

He took several deep breaths of fresh air, and turned round.

He saw the tremendous bulk of the American man silhouetted against the light of the pub, fifty yards away.

'Now,' said Julian, 'if you are here to apologize for the War of 1812, I'm prepared to listen . . .'

The shape came forward until it was towering over him. Then it emitted a low, animal growl.

'Just *look* at those stars,' said Anne wonderingly. 'There's nothing like the night sky in Dorset, is there?'

'Do you think Julian will be all right?' asked Dick for the third time, looking over his shoulder. The pub was long ago lost from view, and Dick was feeling that he had betrayed one of the key responsibilities of the fellow drinker, in leaving his brother to his fate.

'I don't care,' said Anne. 'He's a beast . . .'

As she said the word, there was a rushing noise in the undergrowth nearby and Anne screamed. Dick put his arms around her protectively as a huge shape leapt across their path and, with a loud snorting of animal breath, disappeared into the distance with a great shaking of branches.

'It's okay,' Dick said. 'It's gone.'

'What was it?' whispered Anne.

'A dog,' said Dick. 'Just a dog.'

'That dog's been *working out*,' said George.

'It was a dog,' said Dick. 'We startled it, and because we couldn't see it, we imagined it to be bigger than it was. But it was a dog.'

'Hey,' said Anne, pointing across the sky. 'Look.'

'What?' asked George, grateful that Anne was changing the subject. 'What is it?'

'A full moon.'

On the remainder of their journey, there were no more sudden shocks, but by now they were jumping at every small rustle in the undergrowth.

All the local woodland wildlife seemed to be awake and

calling to each other. Almost, Dick thought, as though the animals were scared of something . . .

When they turned the final corner and saw Kirrin Cottage ahead of them, they felt the relief of being home, and safe. George started fishing in her pocket for the keys.

It was at that moment that the longest and loudest howl any of them had ever heard went up from nearby. For a long, cold moment, they were transfixed by sheer terror, and it was only when they took possession of their faculties again that they grasped just how near the sound had been. It felt like it had come from barely a dozen yards away.

Even George screamed – and then they all sprinted, flat out, for the door. After a few interminable and unbearable seconds of slippery handedness with the keys, the door was open and they were inside. Then it was shut and they were all leaning on it, heaving enormous breaths.

'Even if that's not a werewolf,' said Anne, 'it's a pretty bloody dangerous wolf all right.'

'Whatever it is,' Dick said, 'it's not good. Anne – let's barricade the doors and windows.'

'Okay,' said Anne.

'I'll get the gun,' said George.

For the second time in a minute, the other two screamed.

'What?' George asked. 'Don't overreact. We're in the country. People have guns in the country. Daddy inherited the gun from his father – a historical fowling piece. Still works, though. That's why the pigeon population of Dorset is at an all-time l—'

At this point, the door thundered nearly off its hinges under an attack from outside. Anne screamed, while Dick threw himself against the door with all his strength. There was a brief interlude of gasping, during which the door suffered no further attacks, and Timmy barked his head off. Anne and Dick turned to find George staring at them, wide eyed.

'*Get the gun*,' said Anne.

George ran to lock Timmy safely upstairs, and then reach the gun down from its case, while Anne and Dick grabbed a nearby dresser and pulled it up against the door.

This accomplished, brother and sister set about piling items of furniture against the windows. There was another crash against the front door, as strong as the first, but by now Dick and Anne were so terrified that they didn't even comment on it. They moved with concentrated swiftness,

When they turned the final corner and saw Kirrin Cottage ahead of them, they felt the relief of being home, and safe.

knowing that their lives depended on the actions of every precious second.

'Where is it?' asked George, coming into the kitchen and finding her cousins hunkered down behind the kitchen table, which they had turned on its side.

'We don't know,' said Anne. 'There's not been a sound for a while . . .'

As she said this, there was a tinkle of glass from the living room. They all held their breath.

'He won't get in there,' said Dick. 'All the windows and doors on the ground floor are fully blocked. We did them all.'

'Good,' said George. She was concentrating fiercely as she fiddled with the gun, swearing under her breath as her nervous fingers refused to do her bidding. At last, she cocked the hammer back. It was now fully loaded.

'I've got an idea,' said Dick. He scurried forward on all fours to the kitchen door, and removed the armchair they had pressed against it.

'What are you doing?' whispered Anne.

'If he's determined to get in, he will eventually. If we make sure he comes in this way, we can have a shot at him.' Dick hurried back to join the others.

Realizing that, if Dick's plan worked, she'd definitely have to use the gun, George's hands trembled crazily. She took deep breaths, letting them out slowly to try and get her pulse under control.

There had been no follow-up noise from the living room. They assumed he had found there was no access there, and must be continuing his way round the house.

Against the light of the full moon, they now saw a shadow fall across the kitchen window.

'Oh God,' said George. 'Oh God, oh God.'

The shadow passed beyond the window. Then, a moment later, the kitchen door rattled loudly.

'NOW!' shouted Anne and Dick together.

There was a deafening boom in the small enclosed kitchen, which vibrated up off the stone floor and down off the timbered ceiling, pulverizing their ears. The room filled with smoke and breaking glass for a few moments, and, when they could see again, they saw that the kitchen door had been torn to shreds.

An enormous hole had been blasted through its centre, leaving it hanging in two halves from separate hinges. Beyond it, there was nothing to be seen.

Then a voice carried across to them through the ringing of their eardrums.

'What the FUCK?! You've . . . You've *shot* me!'

'Julian!' screamed Anne, jumping up and running over to the door. 'Oh my God, I'm so sorry! We thought you were that terrible ma— *Oh* my *God*!' This final remark was in response to catching sight of Julian, lying flat out on the back step, and what had happened to his midriff.

His shirt had fared considerably worse than the door, and had been torn away almost entirely. The rest of his tummy was a mess of wood splinters and blood.

'Don't just stand there, dear girl,' Julian said with surprising gentleness. 'Help me inside? There's a madman on the loose out here . . .'

Together they half-carried, half-dragged a whimpering Julian into the kitchen, trailing blood all the way. They propped him up against the kitchen table and looked at his stomach, wondering what any of them could or should do to help.

'If a situation ever called for brandy,' Julian observed, 'this is it. Hand it over, will you, Dick? Thanks. Oh, that's better. God, do I feel sorry for the pigeons of Dorset.

But, look, don't worry about me – I can call myself an ambulance. Save your bloody selves – that lunatic is out there somewhere. Get that door protected.'

'Of course,' said George. 'I'll reload the—'

And here George let out her second scream of the evening.

Turning, she saw that, in her hurry to help Julian, she had dropped the shotgun in the kitchen doorway. Which was now filled by the enormous American, with his foot pressed firmly on the gun's stock.

He was twitching and shuddering with fury. They all looked up at him, petrified.

'What is your *problem*?' he roared.

They had nothing to say. They simply looked at him.

'I just wanted to ask you guys something!' he said. 'I wasn't trying to make trouble. I wanted to meet some locals. And this asshole started to try and fight me!' He looked around at the furniture pressed up against the windows. 'What the hell is going on? What are you *doing* here like this?'

'We thought you were the wolfman,' said Julian, dribbling blood down his chin.

'The *what*?'

'Well, you do look a little bit . . . wolf*ish*,' suggested Dick.

This caused the American to look down at himself. 'I guess,' he said, 'a bit. But I heard you all talking about an American base near here during the war, and I just wanted to ask you about it. I've had a few drinks, I'll admit – but only because no one would talk to me. I've been here looking for my grandfather.'

'Your grandfather?' said Anne.

'He was stationed here in the war,' the American said. 'Seems what he was working on was top secret, and I can't find out what it was. But we know he went missing, near to that pub. And I just wanted to find out what happened to h—'

He was cut off by a sound. A deep, rumbling, gurgling sound. A sound of tremendous power and malice that rippled out of the darkness.

'What the h—' the American began, turning to look out into the night. But he was cut off again, this time by his own scream. Something heavy leapt from the shadows and seized hold of his leg.

The Kirrins inside the cottage caught nothing except a blur of silver hair and the flash of white teeth. They got the sense of an enormous beast, several times larger than the largest wolf they had ever seen. But the room was filled with smoke, their minds fevered with adrenalin, and the activity was taking place beyond the reach of the kitchen light – so it was hard to tell if they saw anything at all.

What they could see was the American on his back, screaming, as something terrible was being done to him. The night was filled with the snarl and squelch of tearing flesh, and the wet crunch of bones. The ordeal lasted less than thirty seconds, during which the Kirrins did not dare to breathe.

The young man's screams trailed away as though he was being dragged off into the night.

Then there was silence.

Slowly, they all started to breathe.

Then Anne had a thought.

'Didn't Aunt Fanny and Uncle Quentin say they wanted the house spick and span when they returned?' she asked. She looked at her phone. 'Which is in . . . six hours?'

Everyone screamed again.

CHAPTER TWO

'How do you like that?' Anne asked. 'Nice and relaxed now, are you?'

Dick and George had thoroughly enjoyed Anne's rendition, and announced that it was a jolly good horror story. Julian, affecting not to be scared, said that it was preposterous, and one shouldn't go around telling such silly stories, as they were not in the least bit frightening. Then he yelped at a nearby sound, which turned out to be a log rolling over in the fire.

'I didn't like the portrayal of Julian, either,' he said. 'I didn't feel it was true to life. He seemed to me a little foolish, and rather pompous. And this insinuation that he drank that much, on a regular basis – I mean, it's—'

'There are no ciders left,' said Dick.

'*What*?'

'Only joking,' said Dick.

'Don't play with my feelings like that,' said Julian, snatching the bag from him.

'So, are we about ready for bed, then?' Anne asked.

'Never felt so far away from sleep, myself,' said George. 'Especially now the fire's dying down. I'm *freezing*.'

'Me too,' said Dick. 'I'd rather warm up by walking than stay here.'

Julian had been shivering for other reasons while Anne's tale was unfolding. He readily agreed with the others.

'I'm sure we'd be nice and warm if we could find some proper shelter,' said Anne.

'How about that church we passed yesterday?' said Julian. 'Even if it's locked, we could probably camp out in the porch.'

Although the others were all rather enjoying the fact that Julian was patently terrified, they couldn't ignore the fact that it was starting to creep up on them too. The nearby woodland was thronging with life, and the night air with filled with rustling, shrieking and all sorts of animal noises, which, accompanied by the occasional hoot, left them feeling far from restful. A shortish hike towards some sign of civilization seemed rather a good idea.

*The American visitor was a truly remarkable specimen, and
practically oozed testosterone. He made Hugh Jackman
appear positively girlish by comparison.*

This agreed, they struck camp with impressive speed and set off across the fields in the direction in which Julian insisted the church lay.

While they walked, a ground mist rose around them, which made it hard to navigate and rendered the sounds of the surrounding wildlife more frightening and disorientating than before.

Still, as they crossed stiles, trudged across fields and clambered over gates, Julian insisted that he knew the way.

When they came across a stone wall and, searching along it, descried a gate, for the first time it occurred to the others that Julian might actually have been right all along. They pushed open the gate and, among swirling tendrils of mist, found themselves in a graveyard.

'Spooky,' said Dick. 'Well done, Jules.'

'I've never been in a graveyard at night,' said Anne.

'Charming, isn't it?' said Julian. 'Mind out for used johnnies, I know what these locals are like.'

'You are the most disgusting . . .' said Anne, her voice trailing off as she looked under her feet.

Dick bumped into George's back, and nearly swore, but saw she was holding up a hand.

'What?' he asked.

'*Ssshhhhh*,' she whispered. 'I saw something.'

'Yeah, I can see loads of things in this moonlight,' said Julian. 'There're tombstones, and trees, and a church steeple—'

'Shut up,' murmured Anne. 'I saw it as well.'

'*Grrrrrrr*,' said Timmy.

'You be quiet, too,' George said to him. 'I hate to hurt your male pride, but you're a hundred and ninety years old in dog years, and you're not going to save us from anything. What was it, Anne? The shape of a man, right?'

Anne nodded. 'I think so. He went that way. Let's go the other way round the church, see if we can get a look at him.'

The boys were far from convinced that the apparition was real. But they also knew that by now the group had scared themselves to the point where panic was but a poorly timed yelp away. So they kept their silence and followed Anne and George as they trod carefully forward, their footsteps muffled by the thick coating of autumn leaves.

The church steeple rose out of the mist in front of

'Go and get your head pummelled in then, Julian!'
Anne said. 'See if I care.'

them, a gaunt and pitiless façade that, now they set eyes on it, made them feel somehow further from the embrace of civilization than ever. Julian wondered why sacred buildings had to be adorned by such things as gargoyles, and, regarding the diabolic artistry of their design, he also wondered whether the carving of them came as a cruel burden to the pious stonemason, or, to the impious one, a rare holiday from otherwise uniform tasks . . .

'*Hurry up,*' said George, yanking his sleeve.

'I was having a profound thought about architecture,' said Julian.

'Well, do that in your own bloody time,' she said. 'For now, just keep up with us and don't say a damn word.'

They all inched forward in a line, with Anne at the front, creeping around the right side of the church. Dick and Julian were starting to feel this was all a tad melo-dramatic, as Anne reached the final buttress and peeped round.

She looked back at the others and shook her head, as though to say the coast was clear.

'Where's Timmy?' whispered George.

They all looked around, and at that moment a gentle

33

stirring of wind lifted the curtain of mist not twenty feet in front of them. They saw, first, Timmy, sniffing around in the grass, and then, as the mist cleared further, a figure behind him.

It was a resolutely human figure, as thick and large as life, yet outlined only in darkness. His arms were raised above his head, and in them was an implement of violence, a weapon held up to its greatest height and about to strike.

The cousins all simultaneously yelled and ran forward.

'Woof!' said Timmy, so startled he jumped and span around three times. 'Woof! Woof!'

When they reached the dog, the figure in the mist beyond had disappeared.

'My darling boy,' said George, cuddling his neck and covering his forehead with kisses. 'What are you doing? Who was that man?'

'If it *was* a man,' added Anne.

'Where did he go?' asked Dick.

Then, looking around, their eyes fell on an open grave nearby. And, in that instant, a spectre rose out of it. A shape covered in dirt, his arms outstretched, and with all the fury of hell upon his visage.

They all screamed as they had never screamed in their lives.

'What the bloody hell do you think you're doing here?' bellowed the man. He put his meaty hands on the edge of the grave and hauled himself up, then stood there, brushing loose earth off himself. This accomplished, he turned his incredulous gaze upon the intruders.

'*Well*?' he asked.

'We could just as well ask the same question of you!' Julian said.

The man squared up to Julian (he was six inches taller), and looked down at him.

'I'm doing my job,' he said. 'I'm getting the graves dug as have to be dug.'

'You might do it in daylight, rather than scaring innocent people half to death,' suggested Anne.

'Have you tried to put a daughter through university on a gravedigger's wage?' he asked. 'Have you? No, I guessed not. Weekdays, I'm a landscape gardener; week-ends, I work split shifts as the barman in the Griffin, down at the bay. Night-times, when the work comes along, I do this.'

'Ah,' said Dick. 'Well. Good for you.'

'It ain't bloody good for me, not when I get groups of arrogant little posh prats coming out of nowhere in the middle of the night, scaring me into the grave,' he said. 'You *actually* scared me into a grave! God, look at these sleeves. What are you doing out here, anyway?'

George stepped forward. 'I'm George,' she said. 'And we're really sorry. We really didn't mean anything by it.'

'You see, we've scared ourselves shitless by telling ghost stories,' explained Julian.

'One ghost story,' said Anne.

'So we're a tad jumpy,' Julian went on.

'We've got ciders,' said George. 'If you want one?'

'Oh, are you sure?' Julian asked nervously. 'I thought we'd run out. We're certainly very low . . .'

'All right,' said the gravedigger. 'I can see if you're anything, it's stupid rather than nasty. And it's about time I took a break, anyway. Why don't you come round to the church porch – there are benches, and it's out of the wind. And thanks but no thanks to your cider, I've got a flask of whisky . . .'

'*Wizard*,' said Julian. 'You must be very strong to dig

There was a rushing noise in the undergrowth nearby and Anne screamed. A huge shape leapt across their path and, with a loud snorting of animal breath, disappeared into the distance.

all these graves, and it's so courageous of you to do all this work to put your daughter through university . . .'

'You're not having any whisky,' the man said.

'So, the name's Jaspers,' the gravedigger said, when they were ensconced in the porch, swathed with blankets and sleeping bags, and starting to feel a bit safer and warmer. They all introduced themselves, and the Kirrins explained their travails so far that evening.

Meanwhile, Dick passed round his leftover sandwiches for those who were hungry, and handed out the remaining ciders to himself, George and Julian. Jaspers turned down the food and took a hefty swig from his hip flask.

'Do you ever get spooked, working in such a place?' asked Anne.

'Not really,' said Mr Jaspers. 'There's a legend of a ghost in a white robe who comes out on nights like this and steals people's souls, but I've been working here fifteen years and I've not had so much as an unpleasant shiver. Until you pillocks showed up.'

'Sorry again about that,' said Dick.

'What keeps you so sane?' asked George.

Jaspers took his phone from his pocket and waved it. 'Audio books, innit?' he said. 'I might be digging all night, but doesn't mean I can't improve the old noggin. Last three months, I've been working my way through the Barchester Chronicles by Trollope. Pretty decent stuff. Hey, hands off my skull!'

'Sorry, sorry,' said Julian, who had just discovered a human skull beneath the bench and was playing with it. He handed it over.

'S'all right,' said Jaspers, 'only I keep my baccy in there, where my wife can't find it.' He levered up the top of the skull and dug out his smoking paraphernalia. When he had finished rolling and lighting his cigarette, he held the skull up.

'I knew him,' he said. 'His name was Maurice.'

'Alas, poor Maurice,' said Julian.

'Not really,' said Jaspers. 'He were a right twat. Hey, so, talking of skulls, who fancies a scary story?'

Anne and Dick nodded. They were so wide awake that they might as well be entertained, after all.

'Good,' said Jaspers lugubriously, 'because I have a

story about four youngsters just like yourselves. In fact, I might as well change their names to yours.'

'Woof!' said Timmy.

'Yes, and a dog too,' said Jaspers, ruffling Timmy's neck. 'A dog just like you, lad. Although you're not in it much. This story, it's quite horrible. Bearing in mind your names, I'd call it . . .'

The Picture of Julian Kirrin

'I say, Dick, this might be your greatest painting yet,' said Julian.

The young artist, Dick, who was wont to wear an expression of anguish and self-doubt, smiled diffidently. 'Are you sure?' he asked.

'Quite sure,' said Julian. 'All that is purest and most generous in the beauty of the world is contained in this picture. You have perfected art. In fact, I cannot bear to think of anyone other than me staring upon it . . .'

'Have you two dickheads finished crapping on about paintings?' asked Sir George, a young buck who was Julian's lifelong friend, and who had only lately appeared in London after resigning his commission in the army.

'Er,' stammered Julian, 'how perfectly refreshing it is to have you here, George. Yes. Yes, I suppose we have said all we can say about this picture – which itself says all that *art* can say—'

'Walk and talk,' said Sir George. 'My stomach's rumbling like a bastard over here. The hansom cab is here, the horses are snorting, and pork chops wait for no man . . .'

Julian cast a nervous look in Dick's direction, but the sensitive young artist was, of course, affecting not to hear, sniffing a lilac and looking out at the garden instead. Julian told himself for the third time today that it was salutary to have Sir George around, to remind him of where he came from, and that good manners would rub off on the lad in due course.

'Before we go, Dick, my dear boy,' said Julian, 'I wish to purchase this picture. And, what's more, to procure your agreement that it will never be shown to anyone else.'

'But my dear sir—' began Dick.

'I will not hear another word,' said Julian Kirrin. 'You know I have come into some money, and there is nothing I want more than to patronize one of the great talents of our age. This one portrait, I'm afraid, I must keep to myself. Call me selfish, call me vainglorious—'

All the local woodland wildlife seemed to be awake and calling to each other. Almost, Dick thought, as though the animals were scared of something . . .

'I'm calling you late for lunch, dickwad,' said Sir
George.

Julian winced. 'Of course. Just coming. Dick, I insist
you come with us! It will be a feast, and we have much
to celebrate . . .'

At the restaurant, the three young men deposited their
hats and canes, and were shown to the table. Here they
were met by a large collection of their oldest friends, their
newest enemies, and a healthy serving of the season's most
fashionable strangers.

The Dowager Fanny Quirrington, an elderly woman in
possession of new money, was far from fashionable. But
she was so stupendously rich, thanks to being predeceased
by her millionaire husband, the hair-oil baron, that, although
she made no attempt to follow fashion, fashion followed
her. And fashion, today, was to be found in the body of
the young debutante, Lady Anne, daughter of the Earl of
Dorset, who was seated to Lady Quirrington's left.

'Another dozen oysters!' bellowed Lady Quirrington, as
she saw Dick and Julian arriving. The waiter, who was in
the process of laying a platter of oysters in front of her,

observed politely that there were twenty-four oysters at the table already. Lady Quirrington blinked stoutly through her lorgnette, noted that this was the case. But she would not be contradicted by the staff.

'*Two* dozen more then,' she demanded. 'Quick, quick! Don't stand there like a brained trout!'

'My dear Lady Quirrington,' said Julian, taking his seat. 'There is only one thing worse than eating oysters.'

'Oh yes, my dear?' she said, squinting through her eyeglass. 'And what is that?'

'Aha!' said Julian. He noticed that everyone at the table was listening to him. 'Well, now,' he said, looking around at them all. The pulse in his neck beat painfully. 'I should say that it is, ah –' he gulped – 'eating . . . anything else!'

The table erupted in laughter and applause. Julian Kirrin sat back in his chair, trying to take a deep breath without it impeding his supercilious smile. Under cover of eating an oyster, he discreetly dabbed the sweat from his brow.

'I was saying to Mr Dickens just the other day,' warbled Lady Quirrington, 'how a luncheon party simply is not a luncheon party without you, Julian. Was I not, Charles?'

Although the others were all rather enjoying the fact that Julian was patently terrified, they couldn't ignore the fact that it was starting to creep up on them too.

'You were indeed,' said Charles Dickens, looking up from his devilled kidneys.

'Chuck, me old lad!' yelled Julian. 'Didn't spot you there. I say, have you written a novel this morning?'

'Two,' said Dickens, taking a swig of Madeira.

'A HANDBAG?' screamed Lady Quirrington, in reply to a question from a waiter. 'Oh, yes. That is my handbag. Leave it there, thank you.'

'Now,' Julian went on, 'I have an announcement. You see, Dick, here, whom you know I have long considered one of London's most promising painters, has produced a true masterpiece. A work that, if it were seen, would change the art world forever. Therefore, for the good of the art world, and the world in general, I have bought it. And none of you will ever see it.'

'But my dear Mr Kirrin,' said Lady Anne, 'how could you be so selfish, keeping such a thing of beauty to yourself?'

'Not at all,' said Julian. 'I'm thinking of everyone *but* myself. It is so scandalously good that, if allowed into the wild, it would change art forever – turn Rembrandt to ashes, reduce Botticelli and Bellini to mere daubs. I cannot do it to the world.'

'I believe you are brave and foolhardy in equal measure,' said Lady Anne, with desperate emotion.

'To be foolhardy, sometimes is to be brave,' said Julian. 'But to be brave, is never ... is ... er—' His train of thought was broken, at this point, by his friend, Sir George, letting out a long, languorous, trembling belch.

'Are you going to talk total bollocks all evening?' asked Sir George.

'You must forgive my friend,' said Julian. 'He is only lately returned from the battlefield, and has not adjusted to our London ways.'

'I find him quite charming,' said Lady Anne. Julian could see quite clearly that Lady Anne was lying, and that he had his work cut out for him.

'I must say, it seems irresponsible to me, for you to keep the painting,' said a young man, an art critic whom Julian knew only enough to identify him as a Mr Chamberlain.

Julian denied the charge vehemently and, seeing Sir George grow restless once again at the discussion of art, hurried the conversation on to different topics.

When the lunch concluded, after several excellent brandies, Julian went outside to clear his head. His attention was caught by a whistle from a nearby alley and, wandering into the shadow, he discovered the person trying to catch his attention was none other than Chamberlain, the young art critic.

'Well?' Julian asked.

'You'll let me see it, won't you?' asked Chamberlain.

'I BEG YOUR PARDON, SIR?' bellowed Julian.

'The painting,' pleaded Chamberlain.

'Oh,' said Julian, 'that. No. It's out of the question. No one can see it.'

'But I am an art critic!' Chamberlain protested. 'And if your description is accurate, then I *must* see it. In fact, I intend to, by fair means or foul. And I don't think you can stop me . . .'

A few days later it was reported that a certain young art journalist, by the name of Chamberlain, had gone missing. And, just a day later, a most unpleasant discovery was made in the backstreets of the West End. Julian Kirrin's heart quickened as he read the report, and he went over and over the details in his mind.

But each time he tried to recall the conclusion of his

discussion with young Chamberlain, his mind went blank. He simply could not remember it. All he knew was that he had arrived home in a daze, covered with mud and scratches, and so exhausted he had been forced to remain inside for several days.

Frequently, his thoughts turned to the dark possibility – indeed, on the face of it, the *likelihood* – that he had had a hand in the young man's demise. And yet there were so many unanswered questions.

Invitations were always arriving thick and fast, for all London wanted to boast of having had the handsome and urbane Mr Kirrin to their parties. This meant that there were plenty of distractions and, sooner or later, Julian managed to force himself to forget the unfortunate incident with the young art critic. A coincidence, he assured himself. A striking coincidence, no doubt, but nothing more.

That was until a few years later, when the circumstances repeated themselves. There was another art critic by the name of Ian Binnie, who brought up the subject of the mysterious painting. Another blackout. And another grisly discovery . . .

And, after another decade had passed, and Julian had

finally succeeded in suppressing the memory, it happened yet *again* . . .

Twenty-five years passed, during which time Julian continued to walk tall and proud among his peers, respected in the city, much invited and fawned over, and the subject of constant gossip – not least on how it was that, despite the passage of so many years, he had never aged so much as a day.

One happy morning, Julian found himself dressing for a special luncheon party to celebrate the Dowager Quirrington's ninety-fifth birthday. Naturally everyone who arrived at the table claimed to be astounded by Lady Quirrington's appearance, insisting she didn't look a day over seventy.

When it came to Julian's looks, however, people's surprise was genuine.

'My eyes are failing me,' said the now very diminutive Lady Quirrington, on Julian's arrival. 'In fact, they failed me years ago. But I would say you must be Julian Kirrin's son. Am I not right?'

Julian chuckled self-deprecatingly.

'Not one bit. It's still me,' he said.

'Then I don't know what you are taking,' she trilled, 'but please give some to me. While there's time.'

Julian bowed deferentially. 'You are too flattering, my dear lady,' he said. 'But I'm afraid your eyes *are* failing you.'

His nearer and younger companions, however, were not at all convinced. First among them was the young Lady Anne as once was, now long married to the Duke of Essex (a notorious pig), and mother to his seven children. She eyed Julian sharply.

'You've not got so much as an eyelash out of place,' she said. 'And not a wrinkle to be seen. I'd say this was a case of Dr Faustus. Wouldn't you agree, Mr Marx?'

The Germanic-looking man to Anne's left nodded eagerly.

'Oh, *ja*,' he said, nodding. '*Ja, ja! Ist unmenschlich!*'

'It certainly was a most wondrous mystery, those art critics getting murdered,' said a youth at Julian's elbow. 'It must have troubled you a good deal, sir.'

'There is only one thing worse than being troubled,' said Julian, throwing his head back and looking into the distance.

Panic was but a poorly-timed yelp away.

'And what is that?' asked the youngster.

'Being kicked in the bollocks,' said Sir George. There was a small silence at the table, during which Julian made up his mind once and for all not to bring Sir George along to these lunches any longer.

'But you would agree that those deaths are a terrible mystery,' persisted the young man, 'worthy of the great Sherlock Holmes himself?'

'I suppose one might say so,' conceded Julian. 'Would you agree, Sherlock?'

'Hmngh?' said the Great Detective from the other side of the table, through a mouthful of crème brûlée.

'I suppose they'll never truly be solved,' said Julian, feeling, as he said the words, the awful drip-drip-drip of guilt through his entire being. His throat tightened, the back of his hands started to sweat and he silently begged for the conversation to move on.

'It's terribly nice of you to ask me back for coffee,' said Dick, as they climbed out of the cab.

'It is an honour that the greatest artist of our age should choose to grace my house with his presence,' said Julian lightly. 'And you too, Sir Geor— Hey! George! Stop screaming at the driver; he can't help the state of the London roads. Please leave the man alone.'

Julian rang the bell and was counting on his fob watch how long it took his footman to answer the door (with a view to fining him if it took longer than twenty seconds, which was his strict rule) when to his surprise someone hailed him from the street. He turned with a frown and saw the impertinent young man who had been next to him at lunch.

'Excuse me, sir,' said the young man apologetically, edging forwards. 'I happened to be passing . . .'

This was a transparent falsehood. Julian Kirrin's house was at the far corner of an exquisitely private square, accessible only via a tortuous sequence of backstreets. What's more, Julian and his companions had driven straight home from lunch, meaning this man must have followed hard on their heels.

Therefore, Julian Kirrin merely regarded the young man with suspicion, and gave no reply at all.

He stammered, 'My name is Simon Greenacre; I am a journalist. And I was hoping to speak to you, sir . . .'

'You are doing so,' said Julian.

'You said you wanted to clear up the mystery of those deaths.'

'I *didn't* say that, as a matter of fact,' said Julian, before adding reluctantly, 'although, naturally, I would like to do so. But how your visiting me uninvited like this can help, I fail to see.'

'I can elucidate,' said the man, venturing to the bottom step. 'You see, I have spoken with the witnesses.'

'Let's go inside,' said Sir George. 'It's cold and I'm bored.'

'Yes, of course,' said Julian, just at the moment that his footman opened the door. He was still chewing, and wore a guilty expression.

'Thought I'd be out longer, did you, Maskell? We'll have words about this. Show us in, prepare our tea and, for God's sake, swallow your lunch. I suppose you may as well join us, sir,' he said to the young man, 'and we can get this over and done with now.'

'It is remarkable,' said Dick, looking over Julian's shoulder a few minutes later, as the latter regarded himself in the ormolu mirror. 'You really *haven't* aged a day.'

'Can't say the same for you, old chap,' said Julian.

Dick acknowledged ruefully that he did not lie. The artist had been living an artist's life, with all that involved, for many decades now. He had enjoyed success too much. He already had a full set of paunches: eyes, chin and stomach. His skin was blotchy and his eyes were almost always pink.

'Dick is right, Julian,' said the young journalist, pouring out the tea. 'It *is* remarkable that you have maintained your looks so exactly, despite your famously whirlwind diary. There's scarcely a social engagement in the metropolis that you aren't invited to, and you scarcely ever miss one.'

'Watch it, mate,' said Sir George, leering at him.

'I'm only desperate to get to the bottom of these killings,' said Greenacre. 'And I feel that I might be close. You see, I believe they are all connected to a portrait that our present artist made all those years ago – one that stands within this very house.'

'I find that hard to believe,' said Julian weakly.

Yet he did believe it.

How long was it since the portrait had been painted? A quarter of a century? And how many art critics had

'Hurry up,' said George, yanking his sleeve.
'I was having a poetic thought,' said Julian.
'Do that in your own bloody time,' she said.

been killed, after mentioning the portrait? Four, by his last count, and who knew if there might not be others . . .

He suddenly made up his mind.

'Perhaps I *have* been selfish all this time,' he said. 'Perhaps I should share it with someone else, after all . . .'

'This is what I was hoping,' said Greenacre, 'so I could clear up the mystery! You see, I have a theory . . .'

'Don't do it, Julian,' growled Sir George.

'The truth is,' Julian admitted, 'keeping the picture to myself weighs on me. I've long wanted to share it. With one person, at least. If I can swear you to secrecy . . .'

'Anything,' said Greenacre. 'I give you my word. I just want to see it.'

'You don't object, Dick?' asked Julian.

'Why would I?' said Dick. '*I* don't want the thing to be secret. I never understood why you hid it up in that dusty attic, anyway.'

'Follow me, then,' said Julian. So saying, he led his guests up the stairs to the third floor, and to the door of the attic, recessed in darkness at the furthest end of the corridor. He felt in his pocket for the only key. Unlocking the door, he pushed it open and picked up the candle that stood inside. Lighting it, he proceeded up a far narrower and more rickety staircase.

Dust and cobwebs drifted around them in the candlelight as they climbed.

'It's in the corner,' said Julian, leading the way. 'Is everyone here?'

The journalist, coughing, confirmed that they were.

'You see, people have always wondered about the portrait, and why I keep it secret. Now you will see for yourselves.'

'Don't do it, Julian!' yelled George. 'Things are fine as they are. Don't spoil it!'

But Julian wasn't listening. He moved towards the shroud that covered the picture and, holding the candle up, pulled it away with a flourish. Dust swirled and the candle flickered as all eyes struggled, in the semi-dark, to take the portrait in.

They all stared at it. The art critic let out a squeak.

'I said I kept it secret for the good of art, and the good of London society. And so I did. For I'm sorry to say this, dear Dick, but it was quite your worst.'

'My worst?' Dick asked.

'By some distance. I had always held you in the highest esteem, and I knew you were on the verge of making a name for yourself, and becoming a credit to queen and country. So, in all conscience, once I set eyes on the thing, I could not allow it out of this house. I knew you would improve, and I was right. I did it to protect you.'

This was a bitter blow for poor Dick to receive, and he simply nodded, trying to take it in.

'But I thought all along this was a portrait of you, Julian,' said Sir George, appalled.

'Yes,' said the bewildered journalist. 'I was convinced of it.'

'Oh, no,' said Julian, quite taken aback. 'I commissioned Dick to paint a portrait of my favourite dear hound – name of Timmy. Wonderful dog. But, as you see, something possessed Dick to portray Timmy not as he really was, but anthropomorphised. That is to say: standing up, and playing billiards, with some other dogs, while wearing a hat and smoking a cigar. Now, Dick, why was that?'

Dick shrugged. 'It was an experimental phase I was going through. Didn't last long, I admit.'

Julian turned to the art critic. 'So you understand why I could never show this to the public?'

The critic agreed wholeheartedly. 'Yet . . . this just deepens the mystery,' he said. 'Please, sir – may I confess to you what I *thought* was happening?'

Julian assented.

'Many of us had formed a wild surmise that you had made some sort of . . . dark pact with a, er, perhaps I should say . . . a demonic entity of some sort. Well, Lady Anne put it perfectly herself, just this lunchtime: we all thought the case had a touch of the Dr Faustus about it. We supposed the portrait to be of you – and that *it* was ageing, while you weren't. Now I hear myself say it I confess I see how fanciful it was. I . . . I feel quite foolish and chastened. And yet . . . how, sir, is it that you *haven't* aged?'

'Yes,' agreed Dick. 'Especially considering how much *you* drink. You drink more than me and I'm practically on my last legs, as you've said yourself!'

'What can I say?' Julian said. 'You flatter me. I confess I take the waters regularly in the south of France. I always drink a glass of this new health drink – Coca Cola – before bed. And, of course, I smoke – Dr Pulsifer tells me that it

Unlocking the attic door, Julian proceeded up a far narrower and more rickety staircase.

is so good for one. Apart from that, I suppose I have good genes. As for your condition, Dick, why, you have a wife and ten children. That is where you have gone wrong.'

Dick nodded sadly.

'But that doesn't explain the *central mystery*,' said Greenacre, 'my one reason for suspicion. Those critics who went missing – all killed, and in the most hideous circumstances.'

'Just *leave* it, would you?' asked Sir George, who was getting rather hot under the collar at all this talk of murder and killing. He didn't know why, but he found his temper considerably worsening and the blood starting to rush in his ears. He loosened his necktie and noticed he was breathing hard, and sweat was pouring from his temples.

'I do recall those killings,' Julian admitted. 'And, yes, I confess I was nearby on each occasion. Of course, this has caused me a good deal of puzzlement over the years . . .'

'There is one possible solution,' said the critic. 'The only other person who was there each time was yourself, Sir George . . .'

Sir George, who was standing back from the others and in shadow, growled. It was a deeper and more aggressive growl than the human voice could normally achieve. Yet the others didn't notice; they were too gripped by the unfolding logic of what young Greenacre was saying.

'*I said leave it,*' said Sir George. His voice was barely recognizable – it sounded as wild and threatening as the roar of a lion.

'The question stands,' said Greenacre, nervously peering into the shadow where he knew Sir George stood – a shadow that was rippling with strange animal sounds.

'But my dear sir!' laughed Julian. 'It's perfectly preposterous. What could possibly lead you to suspect my dear friend Sir George Jekyll?'

At that moment, a gust of air blew out the candle. There was the sound of something enormous moving in the attic, and Dick and Julian were both knocked flying. They crashed to the floor, quite unconscious.

The critic turned nervously, first left, then right. In the sudden darkness, he could not see the way to escape.

Then an enormous hand fastened itself around his neck, and he felt the hot breath of snorting nostrils move up close to his ear.

'Julian wasn't the only one protecting his friend . . .' said a voice. It was the voice of Sir George no longer, but that of some primordial beast, a creature of unquenchable rage.

The journalist tried to beg for his life, but the beast was not interested in anything he had to say.

Instead, the fist around his neck suddenly tightened with all its strength. There was a horrible, dense crunching sound, and then there was silence in the attic, broken only by the creature's breathing.

CHAPTER THREE

'That was utterly horrible,' said Julian.

'I'm very gratified to hear you say so,' said Jaspers the gravedigger.

'No, I mean it was so *inconsistent*,' Julian said. 'I mean, it's clearly set in the fin-de-siècle world of Oscar Wilde. Yet Charles Dickens died in 1870, Karl Marx in 1881 and Sherlock Holmes is a bloody fictional character. Not to mention the fact that *Dr Jekyll and Mr Hyde* was by Robert Louis Stevenson . . .'

'Please yourself,' said Jaspers. 'Passed the time, though, didn't it?'

'Tell me again about the ghost that is said to stalk the graveyard at night,' said Dick.

'Well, it has a long, flowing gown, and it drifts along, accompanied by an ethereal light . . .'

'You mean like that?' Dick pointed.

Jaspers screamed. Anne screamed. The white shape screamed.

'Oh, hello, Vicar,' said Jaspers, recovering himself.

'What the devil do you mean by infesting my grave-yard at this ungodly hour?' yelled the vicar, pulling his nightshirt around him. 'Oh, it's you, Edward. Doing a spot of overtime, are you? Well, I'm grateful, of course, but I do wish you could keep it down. A man has to sleep. Ah! And you have some friends . . . Well, it's a relief, I suppose, that you weren't talking to yourself.'

The four cousins introduced themselves and, when the vicar saw what nicely behaved young people they were, he began to regret his harsh words.

'I say, it *is* cold out here,' he observed. 'Why don't you come next door? A tot of sherry might warm us all up . . .'

'Wahey!' said Julian. 'God bless . . . er, well, God. I always said vicars and churches were smashing.'

'You seem like you've had a fair amount already,' commented the vicar, after which Julian kept his thoughts to himself.

*

'Tell me again about the ghost that is said to stalk the
graveyard at night?' asked Dick.

'It's most awfully kind of you,' said Anne, when they were all sat in the cosy front room of the vicarage and the fire in the grate was being urged back to life.

'Not at all,' said the vicar. 'My wife's away, you see. When one's awake on nights like this, it can get quite eerie.'

'We've been telling each other horror stories,' said George, 'to pass the time and keep us warm.'

'Ah, now,' said the vicar, 'scary tales are another thing entirely. They positively cheer me up – don't know why. M. R. James is a particular favourite.'

'Could you tell us one, perhaps?' Dick suggested. 'Thanks for the sherry, by the way.'

'Not at all; it's a pleasure. We've got barrels of the stuff here. For some reason, it's one of the only things people ever give vicars. Heaven forfend I might get something I actually want. Like a good Blu-ray, or a new wok. *Oh* no. But I digress. Yes – a horror story. I have just the thing. It's not the sort of tale you'd usually expect to hear from a vicar, I suppose. But here goes. I call this one . . .'

In Dorset, People Can Hear You Scream

In space, however, they cannot.

The 4551-class space-freight vessel, chartered by the Weymouth-Yatani Corporation (the vicar told them), was nineteen weeks into its long haulage trip back to Earth, after picking up crew members and cargo from a base on an asteroid at the fringes of the Kuiper Belt. The crew of ten were enjoying dinner together in the canteen after what was, by their standards, a spectacularly eventful day.

That morning they had picked up a signal from an unmanned mining vessel that had become stranded. They had altered course to board the vessel, the cargo of which they had salvaged. Now they had finished transporting the cargo (which was of no class or marking they recognized) to their own vessel and making it safe, they were celebrating the prospect of a healthy bonus at the end of their trip.

'Here's to Anne,' said Julian, 'who noticed the signal in the first place!'

A cheer went up around the table. Crew members raised their beers. Anne merely gave a brief nod in acknowledgement, and did not touch her own drink. As Julian went to take a gulp of his, he felt a terrible tearing sensation in his gut.

'Ugh,' he said, doubling over. He slammed down his cup, spilling half its contents, and put a hand to his stomach.

'What is it?' asked George. 'Julian! What's wrong?'

Instead of answering, Julian sprawled on the dining table, knocking bottles and plates on to the floor. Everyone gathered round, terrified.

Julian gasped, clutching his gut. His face was red. Then he rolled from the table, grabbed a nearby bin and retched into it.

'God,' he said, wiping his mouth, 'how many times do I have to tell you, Dick? Before you dish it up you have to check that the food is *piping hot throughout*! That's not just a bloody serving suggestion! You could have given me food poisoning!'

'Sorry,' said Dick. 'I thought I did check.'

'I said it was risky trying to eat lobster thermidor in space,' said George. 'Celebration or no celebration, it's still two-year-old shellfish. I don't care how carefully it was frozen.'

Julian sat back on his chair, looking exhausted, and reached for a swig of beer to clear his mouth.

Before it touched his lips, however, a klaxon sounded, and the consoles on the walls around them were lit up by red flashing lights. The flight officers all got up and watched as Anne consulted the screen.

'What is it?' asked George, as Anne read the screen.

'An unidentified vessel is docking with ours,' said Anne. 'Unscheduled, and I can't make out the identification.'

They all looked at each other.

'Suit up, weapons ready,' said George, 'and let's go to investigate.'

The loading bay was at the far end of the ship, which meant a long trek down many dark passageways. All the crew (except for Anne, who would oversee the expedition from the bridge and remain on coms) donned protective clothing. Then they advanced, in formation, into the belly of the ship.

*'Well, that was a horrible story,' said Anne.
'Don't you agree?'*

George told herself, for the fifth time, that there was nothing to be frightened of. Whatever was going on, it would have a perfectly innocent explanation – despite the fact that she'd never heard of an unidentified craft force-docking with a merchant ship like this one, without warning. She felt a bead of sweat trickle down her forehead to her nose, where she wiped it off with the back of her wrist.

After ten minutes of marching, the crew reached the central nexus of the ship, with passages fanning out in many directions. Here, the route to the rear of the ship divided in two, and they decided they had better cover both approaches. The crew split in half, with Julian, George and Dick going left, and the rest of the crew going right.

Anne gave them updates over their headsets, revealing that the scan of the incoming vessel had been inconclusive.

'There's some movement,' she said. 'But I'm not sure it's a life form. Or at least, not a life form as we identify it.' Scarcely had she finished speaking when the sound of screaming was heard from somewhere within the ship. It was the screaming of multiple voices, all in extreme terror – voices which were cut off, one by one.

'Anne!' Dick yelled over his headset. 'What the hell was that?'

'I'm not getting any visuals,' Anne's voice said calmly in his ear, 'but, from their vitals, it seems several crew members have suffered serious injuries. I'll update you when I know more . . .'

'Jesus,' said Julian. 'What the hell is going on?'

'Stay calm,' said George. 'Could be anything – a mal-function, anything.'

They progressed along the corridor slowly, moving with great caution, weapons raised. At last, as they reached the far end, the ship opened out into the cargo bay. Here, they covered each other, taking extreme care around corners.

'I'm picking up movement ahead of you,' said Anne.

They advanced into the cargo bay, inch by inch, lighting it up with the torches at the end of their pulse canons and finding nothing out of the ordinary. As they progressed, they got more and more jumpy, desperate to finally con-front whatever was awaiting them. Finally, they formed a semicircle around the airlock that connected with the docking bay. Dick reached out and punched a button, and the twin doors swooshed apart, steam jetting from above and below.

Dick, George and Julian gripped their weapons tightly to their shoulders. The steam disappeared and they blinked, trying to accustom themselves to the dark.

'There's nothing here,' said Dick.

'Shhhh . . .' murmured Julian, his trigger finger twitching. 'I saw something!'

There was movement in the darkness. Something small inched towards them, out of the hold. It was knee-high, covered with fur, and blinked out at them with big eyes.

Dick and Julian went down on one knee, weapons still raised.

George moved forward, until she was a few feet away from it. Then she knelt.

'George! What are you doing?' asked Julian.

But George couldn't help herself. It was one of the cutest things she'd ever seen and she felt a strong desire to pet it.

'What *is* it?' asked Dick.

'It looks like an auto-dog,' said George. 'I saw them in the shops before we left. Hey, there's a label.'

'What does it say?' asked Julian.

George touched the heart button at the centre of the label, and suddenly Aunt Fanny's voice filled the cargo bay.

'HELLO, DARLING GEORGIE!' she said. 'I know you'll think me terribly frivolous, but I just couldn't let your birthday – well, birthdays, in fact – go by without sending you a present. I know how much you miss your beloved Timmy, who's safe here with us. And, when I saw this, I couldn't resist having it delivered to you, express. I know it's extravagant, but, for this once, I just thought – blow the expense! I hope you adore it. With all our love – do you send love, Quentin?' There was an inarticulate grunt in the background. 'Of course he does. Bye, darling!'

George, Dick and Julian looked at each other.

'*Mad*,' said George. 'What am I supposed to do with this bloody thing on the ship?'

'Woof,' said the auto-dog.

'Not that I'm not pleased to have you,' George said, giving him a ruffle behind the ears. 'Of course I am.

78

It's terribly nice of Grandma to send you, isn't it? How realistic your fur is . . .'

'Guys!' said Flight Officer Farrelly, coming round the corner from the other end of the bay. 'You're safe! Thank God. Did you see that thing?'

'What thing?' asked Julian.

'*This* thing?' asked George, holding up Timmy 2.0 (as she'd already decided to call him).

'*What*? No, not that,' said Farrelly. 'The thing that attacked us! It got Wong, Ginzberg and Farook. It's huge, and it moves like lightning. After it got them, it vanished up into the ventilation shaft. It might be heading for the bridge. We've got to warn A—!'

He stopped talking as he felt something punch him in the back. He looked at his crew mates again, and saw their expressions. They were no longer looking at him, but above his head, and their faces had grown pale with terror. Farrelly felt something cold and liquid pouring over his neck and shoulder – a substance that looked like motor oil mixed with egg white, and smelled like nothing on earth.

With calm objectivity Farrelly then looked down at the spike protruding from his stomach, and then up at the alien's open mouth. From within it, another mouth emerged, skeleton teeth chittering and cascading with drool.

Julian, Dick and George all fired their weapons at the alien's head. They retreated as fast as they could from the cargo bay, back down the passage they had just used. George carried Timmy 2.0 in her arms.

Running all the way, in a few minutes they reached the central nexus once again.

Julian was surprised that the corridor to the bridge had been closed off.

'Open the bridge-bay doors, Anne,' he said.

'I'm afraid I can't do that, Julian,' said Anne calmly.

'What?' asked Dick. 'That thing is coming after us! Closing the doors won't protect you – it uses the ventilation system! Quickly! It'll be here in seconds! Open the bridge-bay doors!'

'I'm sorry,' said Anne, in exactly the same voice. 'I can't do that.'

There was the sound of distant feet hammering along the metal floor of the pipes that led to the nexus. They were getting closer, fast.

'I can't help feeling the edge has gone off
this camping lark,' said Julian.

'Quickly – to the living quarters,' said George. 'This door is open!'

They leapt through to the living quarters, swept the area to check the coast was clear, sealed the outer and inner doors, and then collapsed, panting. The ship's living quarters formed a separate section of the ship, sealed with double airlocks at each end, so it could detach in case of emergency.

'Anne,' said George, on the radio, 'do you copy? You're in danger! There's a monster aboard. We're safe for now, but it might be coming for you at any second!'

'And what's this about not letting us into the bridge?' asked Dick. 'We were trying to protect you!'

'Guys,' said Anne placidly. 'In fact, it was me who was trying to protect *you*.'

They turned, and saw that Anne had patched a video of herself through to a screen on a wall behind them. For some reason, she seemed chillingly calm.

'Seriously, Anne,' Dick shouted. 'You've got to get out of there. Come and join us in the living quarters!'

'Try to stay calm,' Anne said, 'and listen. I want you to be aware that I have some disturbing news.'

'Anne?' Julian asked. 'Why aren't you running? You'll be killed!'

'Before dinner, I finished analysing the cargo we salvaged from the mining vessel this morning. What I discovered was most impressive. The cargo itself is useless, but within it was a batch of eggs that (all the evidence indicates) belong to a creature from a non-terran civilization. Even from a cursory inspection I can tell that this material will be of incalculable value to the Weymouth-Yatani Corporation. And in such circumstances I'm afraid my key objective is to return it to the corporation intact, for study. At any expense. That overrides all my other orders.'

'But you'll be *killed*!' said George. 'You won't last ten seconds against that thing. It's a machine!'

'Woof!' said Timmy 2.0 aggressively.

'I see you've got a dog,' said Anne.

'It's an auto-dog,' said George. 'A present from Mummy and Daddy. He's called Timmy 2.0.'

'Woof!' protested Timmy 2.0.

'Sorry, darling, I won't call you that again. You're a real dog. And my special little chap, aren't you?'

'How nice,' said Anne.

'Woof!' said Timmy 2.0.

'I'm impressed how many different woofs he has,' said Dick.

'Yes, me too,' said Julian. 'It's more than the real Timmy, isn't it?'

'*Guys*,' said Anne. 'Please. You're not listening. I have to tell you I'm about to cast you loose from the main vessel. This is for your own safety. In the crew quarters there's enough food to last you for more than twenty years. But, with your distress signal sounding, especially on a popular shipping route like this, you should be picked up in less than two. I hope you know that, after all the time we've spent together, it causes me great distress to do this—'

'Not nearly as much distress,' Julian politely pointed out, 'as the enormous creature that just unfurled itself from the ceiling!'

Anne hesitated.

'Behind you,' added George.

'Really,' said Anne. 'I think we're a bit old for those sort of games, are we not?'

Anne became aware of certain noises nearby. She went still. Then she refocused at her three crewmates.

'I may have made a small miscalcul—' she said, before being grabbed and torn in half by the alien creature as it emitted a soaring, split-toned, high-pitched shriek.

Julian, Dick and George all looked away. George covered Timmy 2.0's eyes.

'This is most unfortunate,' said Anne.

'She's still alive!' yelled Dick. They all looked up to see the alien creature slide-scurrying from the bridge. On the floor was Anne's torso and head. Six feet away were her legs. In the space between the two, the floor was covered with wild splashes of white liquid.

'My God!' said Julian. 'I should have known! Anne-droid!'

'Now you mention it,' said Dick, 'I should have guessed when I saw on the roster that her surname was Mark 5.105-v.'

They watched as the mechanoid Anne dragged her top half across the floor and, with great effort, heaved herself up on to the console. 'Pressing the release now, for the living quarters to separate from the main ship. I'm

There was much kissing and tearful waving as the
youngsters got into the car and started the engine.

sorry about this. Good luck. Locks released. Boosters activated . . .'

The screen blinked out.

'What a rotter,' said Dick.

'Woof!' said Timmy 2.0.

'I suppose it was rather decent of her to make sure we actually got away, though,' said George. 'Now, we're stuck here for the foreseeable. Do we know what we actually have to entertain ourselves with?'

'You've got Timmy 2.0,' Dick observed.

'Yes, I have, haven't I? Haven't I, my special boy?'

'Woof! Woof!' said Timmy 2.0.

'I suppose we'll get used to that sort of soppy rubbish with time,' muttered Julian, looking at a map of the living quarters. 'Well, the good news is that we've got a pool, and a gym, *and* a sauna. Look what programmes they've got – we can go running in the Alps, or swimming in Bermuda. That's pretty good. And, hey, look here! There's a library which contains the entirety of Western literature!' He was holding up a tablet about the size of a paperback. 'I've always dreamed of being stuck with nothing to do but hang around and read everything.

Think I'll start with the *Epic of Gilgamesh* and work my way forward . . .'

'And there's the captain's supply of wine,' Dick said. 'Don't you remember? You kept going on at Captain Farook about it, saying it would only go off if we didn't drink it?'

Julian dusted his hands with an expression of supreme smugness. 'All this, and hammocks too. What bliss!'

'George has the dog, you have your books, but what about me?' asked Dick.

Julian slid open a storage unit beneath the large screen. 'Weymouth-Yatani downloads every new video game released, and supplies an omni-console to play them on. We didn't want to tell you before, because we wanted you to get some work done.'

'Amazing!' said Dick, settling into his hammock. 'Do you fancy playing co-op *Far Cry 25* with me?'

'I suppose so, whatever that means,' said Julian. 'You know, I think this might be the best thing that's ever happened to us. Don't you agree, Timmy 2.0?'

'Woof!' said Timmy 2.0. 'Woof! Woof!'

CHAPTER FOUR

'Well, that *was* a nasty story,' said Anne, 'but it's nice to have a happy ending now and then. Don't you agree?'

But her brothers had both dozed off.

'You two!' she shouted, making Dick snort awake. 'Right. Thank you, Vicar. You've been so kind, but we really must be going now.'

'Yes, it's getting on for daytime,' said the vicar, yawning. 'I'd better get an hour's sleep before the morning service. Thank you for keeping me company. And I'd better just take, er . . . Oh. The bottle's empty. How impressive.'

Julian started to let out a long, low snore that was interrupted by Dick kicking him in the ankle.

'What? Ow! Where am I? Who the f— Oh, er, hello, Vicar. Thanks for having us, Your Grace. Sorry to have drunk all your sherry, Your Holy Eminence. It was going down so smoothly. Yes, all right, I'm coming. Wait for me!'

They left the vicarage with many more proclamations of thanks, and with Jaspers and the vicar standing at the front door and waving.

Seeing them standing there together, Anne couldn't help but feel a slight twinge of unease. Whether it was in their gestures, or their expressions, or their facial features, there was something about the two men that struck a chord somewhere deep inside her. Not only did they seem oddly similar to each other, she also felt she'd seen them somewhere before . . .

She forced herself to shake the feeling off, and, as they all set off down the road, she waved madly until they were out of sight.

'I can't help feeling the edge has gone off this camping lark,' said Julian.

George agreed.

'Can we go home, Anne?' Dick asked.

'Woof?' suggested Timmy.

Anne felt the same way. They were all tired, and in need of a bath and their own beds. But, for some reason she didn't understand, she strongly resisted the idea of going home.

'Fanny and Quentin specifically asked us to stay away for a few days,' she said. 'It's the least we can do, isn't it? Considering all they do for us.'

'But it *is* weird, though,' said Dick. 'Isn't it? After all, we're tired, damp, getting cold again, and, er . . .'

'A bit tipsy,' admitted Julian, yawning. 'Besides, we can just use the facilities and set up camp further along the cliff, out of sight. They wouldn't begrudge us that, surely? I mean, who've they got visiting? Edward Snowden?'

Anne nodded. It seemed reasonable.

'I know the number of a cab firm in a local village,' said George.

'Oh, he'll never pick us up at this time on a Sunday,' said Anne. She still didn't understand exactly why, but she felt an strong instinctive aversion to going home.

'If he answers, there's a thirty quid tip in it for him,' said Julian, stifling another yawn.

The taxi dropped them a quarter of a mile away from Kirrin Cottage, so they could walk up to the house and if need be, change their mind and go to camp somewhere else.

As they turned the corner of the road and Kirrin Cottage

came into sight, they saw a car parked outside: a battered, cheap estate car, the sort only used by an impoverished pensioner or a bunch of students. Anne led the others into a ditch that ran alongside the road, to prevent their being spotted, in case by chance they saw something they oughtn't.

The others followed unquestioningly, and Anne almost found herself laughing at her own precaution – except then she remembered the inexplicable disquiet she had felt at the prospect of coming back from camping early. That, and the strange congruence of features she had noticed in the faces of Jaspers the gravedigger and the vicar. And their cab driver, now she thought of it. Was she going mad, or were all the people hereabout very closely related?

As they got closer, the front door opened, disgorging a group of young people – three young men, a teenage girl and a dog. No, Anne saw as she peered closer, it was two boys and two girls – only, one of the girls was dressed just like a boy. She shivered.

There was much kissing and tearful waving as the youngsters got into the car and started the engine.

'What the hell is going on?' asked Julian.

'They're coming this way!' said George.
'Quick! Behind this hedge!'

'Those guys look just like us,' said Dick.

'They're coming this way,' said George. 'Quick! Behind this hedge!'

The others all hunkered right down out of sight, but Anne kept her head up as the car went past.

Once more, she experienced the stab of unease she had felt when she saw Jaspers the gravedigger and the vicar standing next to each other. This time it was much worse – a horrible, sickening revelation, which felt like a dagger to the belly.

The boys and girls in that car – all chatting and laughing, blissfully unaware – looked *exactly* like Anne, her brothers and their cousin. Or, at least, she thought, very, *very* like them. The only difference was that they were much younger – perhaps around the age of twenty, while Anne et al. were all approaching their thirtieth birthdays.

Anne was profoundly troubled – more so, she thought, than she'd ever been in her life. She said nothing to the others as they all got up, dusted themselves off and made their way towards the cottage.

George produced her keys, but for some reason Anne reached a hand out to stop her.

'Just wait,' Anne said. 'I've got a strange feeling.'

They moved closer to the house, still crouching out of sight. The boys felt this was rather a fun game, but George had already picked up on Anne's nervousness. She shushed the boys' giggling as they heard another car approaching.

They all peeked out as the car drew up in front of the house. It was a new car, of the latest registration. As the doors opened, out stepped a very old and frail dog, followed by four adults in their thirties. There was something about them which was more solid and confident than the previous batch; they were all rather more individual in their hair and clothing styles.

They ambled to the door and pressed the bell, and, when Fanny answered, there was the same kissing and hugging as before, but less excitable this time – easier, more comfortable. Perhaps less passionate.

These thirty-somethings also all looked and acted exactly like Julian, George, Anne, Dick and Timmy.

Putting their heads down, hoping not to be noticed, the four exhausted and confused cousins just lay there, pressed against the grass behind the hedge. None of them spoke.

Eventually, George sat up and retreated down the slope,

away from the house. Of course, she was the most upset out of all of them – these were her parents, after all. But by now they were all extremely disturbed. The others joined her.

'Let's go this way,' George said. 'Around the side of the hill.'

They all shuffled along in silence. They had always been used to exposing evildoers and underhand goings on, and confronting such matters head on. But here, they instinctively felt, another approach was called for. This was something beyond their understanding. As they reached two large boulders on their path, George said, 'Well, we can't go any further this way. We'll have to go up to the house and see what we can overhear.'

'What are you talking about?' asked Dick. 'Can't you see the path between the rocks?'

George shook her head. She was starting to feel accustomed to big surprises, and so didn't lift an eyebrow when Dick walked straight towards where the two boulders met, and disappeared through. Anne took George's hand and led her forward. George shut her eyes as she approached the optical illusion and, after twenty steps, she opened them again to find herself on the other side.

'When I was a kid, this was always out of bounds,' she said. 'I must have been hypnotized, or, or brainwashed or something, into not seein— *Ohhh.*'

There was silence except for the wind whipping in over the clifftop. Only Timmy, who could not understand what the others saw, made any noise. He ran and jumped over the upright grey stones laid out in strict formation, pausing to leave his mark behind one of them.

'Don't do that, Timmy,' said Anne sadly. 'Show some respect for the dead.'

They were standing on a wide ledge, a hundred yards beneath the cliff. Looking around, the Kirrin cousins realized how carefully it had been chosen. It would be invisible from the sea, from the beach, and from the cliff above, so it was perfect for the use it had been put to: in front of them was a small, secret graveyard. There were several dozen graves dug in the soft cliff-side soil, each marked by a plain stone, engraved with a few words.

George saw one labelled *Julian II – 1951–1989*, and another labelled *Anne III – 1964–2006*.

'So we weren't the first,' said George.

'Seems not,' said Dick. 'It's hard to take in.'

'And you weren't the last, either,' said a voice.

They all turned to find Quentin standing in the gap between the rocks, cutting off their escape. 'I'm sorry you had to find out like this. But tell me – didn't you wonder why you had childhood memories of adventures you went on in the 1940s?'

They should all have attacked him at once. They should have rushed him, pinned him to the ground, given him a sound beating and demanded answers. But the wind had been taken out of them.

'No,' said Dick. 'It never occurs to you to question your memories. They just are.'

Quentin nodded. 'It was the proudest moment of my life, being invited to work on this project: the cloning of humans, perfectly identical and yet infinitesimally different – according to our own requirements.'

George had started crying into her sleeve. Timmy was still running around in the distance, chasing rabbits, and she was glad that at least he didn't have to see her like this.

'It really is a stupendous bit of science,' said Quentin. 'One of a kind. Started during the war, and continuing to this day.'

'What were you trying to achieve?' asked Anne, trembling.

'We've already achieved more than you can imagine,' said Quentin. 'Half of the winners of the Nobel Prize for Medicine in the last thirty years aren't fit to lick my boots. Many of the most effective treatments and drugs on the market have been developed on the back of the research we have done here. You should be proud – incredibly proud. Between us we've saved millions of lives.'

He paused, perhaps waiting for congratulations. 'I know this must be quite a shock,' he added, quietly.

'Wait!' screamed George.

She had set eyes on a nearby gravestone that read *Quentin II – 1913–75.*

'You aren't even the *original Quentin*?' she asked.

He smiled at her.

'My dear girl, how could I be? I'd be about a hundred and thirty. I was honoured to be the third man to take up the job. But I was *your* Quentin.'

'So, nothing was real,' Dick said. 'None of it. None of our adventures.'

'Of course they were,' said Quentin crossly. 'They were

They should have rushed him, pinned him to the ground,
and demanded answers. But they did not have the energy.

the adventures the original kids went on in the 1940s. We implant all those memories in each of you new batches – to encourage you to be the same. They were heroes, those kids. And you are too! You're the same! You're always having new adventures that play into the next generation! Don't you see it's a good thing?'

They looked at him with empty eyes.

'What about the vicar, and gravedigger Jaspers?' Anne asked. 'And cab-driver Dave? They're other clones, aren't they?'

'Well, yes,' admitted Quentin. 'Sometimes it doesn't work out. When they get to adulthood, we realize we've got a defective batch who don't fit in with our objectives. Then we reprogram them, and release them to lead happy, normal lives – as taxi drivers, gravediggers, even vicars.'

'This can't go on,' said George. 'We're ending this now. If we ever had a call to adventure, this is it: to find our freedom from this unnatural tyranny. Julian, the tent! Anne, the rope! And Dick, the cricket bat!'

On cue, Julian, Anne and Dick brandished the tools which they had all been secretly getting ready (while Quentin was busy speechifying) to capture him with.

However, Quentin had talked at such length quite deliberately. For while he detained the young Kirrins, members of the security services had been moving in to surround the area. As Anne, Julian and Dick went to make their move, they each found themselves distracted by a pricking sensation at the back of their neck.

They fell to the ground while George watched.

'Son of a bitch,' she said, reaching a hand up to her own neck. She plucked out a dart and twirled it between her fingers, wonderingly.

'I really am sorry, darling girl,' said Quentin gently, as George slid to her knees, and then slumped on the grass.

'DARLING?' yelled Fanny from the cliff edge above. 'Lunch is getting COLD!'

'Just coming, dear,' Quentin called back. 'Nearly finished!'

'Julian?' said a voice. 'Julian! Wake up, for God's sake!'

'*Hunngh*,' said Julian, sitting up. 'Get off me! What? Who are you!'

'It's me!' said George. 'What's wrong? Did you have a bad dream?'

Julian writhed around in his sleeping bag, looking left and right. All he could see were the walls of a tent. 'Are we alive? And still camping?'

'What else would we be doing?' asked George. 'You dickhead,' she added.

'I was just . . . I'm not sure,' Julian said, sitting up. He rubbed his temples, and then the back of his neck. He thought he felt a little bump on the skin, which might have resulted from the prick of a dart. But then, spending the night in a sleeping bag often brought him out in hives, and god knew what insects there might be in here.

Anne opened the tent flap, allowing a welcome breeze inside, and handed him a mug of coffee. Julian caught a flash of the field beyond and recognized it from the previous day. He felt as though he was starting to breathe again.

He slurped the coffee and put it down, then scrambled out of his sleeping bag, went outside and took a few circuits of the tent, coffee in hand, taking deep breaths. It did feel good.

'You all right?' George asked.

'No! Yes! Fine. Why do you ask? Fine,' he said. 'Tickety-boo.'

'You didn't have a bad dream?' asked Dick.

'Of course not,' said Julian. 'I am a perfectly balanced and stable individual who only has very normal and sensible dreams, thank you.'

The others stirred the fire and looked at each other.

'Why? How about you lot?' asked Julian.

'Nothing, no dreams at all,' said Dick.

'I never dream,' said Anne. 'Never have. I wonder what it's like.'

'Had a totally boring dream myself,' said George doggedly, 'about being normal and not disturbed. It was great, I loved it. Best dream ever.'

The others looked at her dubiously, while she started to pack up her tent.

'How about you, Timmy? Any dreams?'

'*Woof*,' said Timmy.

'Good ones, I'm sure. Chasing butterflies and whatnot. Good dog,' said Julian. 'Fine. So we're all fine. Great! Let's get on our way, don't you think? Everyone feel like a good long hike today?' he asked.

Dick started to kick over the fire while Anne packed up their tent. George drank her last gulp of coffee and flung the dregs into the ashes, then started gathering their litter into a bag.

'Good!' said Julian. 'We're fine! No bad dreams, everything's fine! And it will carry on being fine. We'll keep going. For ever. Or at least for bloody ages. Because everything's fine. Right?'

No one was listening to him, except Timmy.

'Woof!' said Timmy.